I'M GOING TO EAT A POLAR BEAR

KARL NEWSON   NICOLA KINNEAR

I'm hungry!

No, thank you. Fish are **boring!**

And slippery.

And wet.

And fishy!

I want something **new**.

Something **soft** ... and <u>fluffy</u>!

Soft and fluffy? *Hmmm* . . .
I once heard the tale of a soft and fluffy thing. I think it's called . . .

a bolar pear?!

A bolar pear?
Yes! That will fill me up nicely.
I'm going to eat a bolar pear.

GRUERRP!

What if bolar pears are scary?

I'm not scared . . .

I'll eat a friendly one.

Don't worry. I'll find one.
I'm going to eat a bolar pear . . .

What are you doing here?

I'm going to eat a bolar pear.
Are you a bolar pear?
You're not very fluffy . . .

A polar bear?
No, they live a <u>long</u>, <u>long</u>, <u>LONG</u> way over there!

You can't eat a polar bear.
Polar bears are HUGE!

Good. So is my belly.

GRuERRP!

Are YOU a POLAR BEAR?!

You're a long, <u>long</u>, <u>long</u>, <u>LONG</u> way from home!

AT LAST! This must be the place.

But... I can't see a polar bear anywhere!

GRUERRP!

Woah! That was a big rumble! I must be SUPER hungry.

There aren't any polar bears here . . .

not one.

Not even a little one!

Oh well, I guess I'll just go back home . . .

for

fish . . .

Slippery. Wet. Fishy fish . . .

I'm ba**aa**ck!

That was a long, long, long, long, long, long, looong, looong waste of time. There aren't any bolar pears there! Not one. Not even a little one!

What's that behind you?!

What was that thing?

I have absolutely no idea.
But it sure is scared of fish!

Delicious, fishy, fish.

For Mum and Iain xx
K.N.

For my own hungry penguin,
Connah xx
N.K.

© 2025 Quarto Publishing Group USA Inc
Text © 2025 Karl Newson
Illustrations © 2025 Nicola Kinnear

Karl Newson has asserted his right to be identified as the author of this work. Nicola Kinnear has asserted her right to be identified as the illustrator of this work.

Senior Commissioning Editor: Carly Madden
Senior Designer: Mike Henson
Creative Director: Malena Stojić
Associate Publisher: Rhiannon Findlay
Senior Production Controller: Elizabeth Reardon

First published in 2025 by Happy Yak,
an imprint of The Quarto Group.
100 Cummings Center, Suite 265D
Beverly, MA 01915, USA.
T (978) 282-9590 F (978) 283-2742
EEA Representation, WTS Tax d.o.o., Žanova ulica 3,
4000 Kranj, Slovenia.

www.quarto.com

No part of this publication may be reproduced, stored in a retrieval system, or transmitted in any form, or by any means, electrical, mechanical, photocopying, recording or otherwise, without the prior written permission of the publisher or a licence permitting restricted copying.

All rights reserved.

ISBN: 978 0 7112 9574 2
eISBN: 978 0 7112 9575 9

9 8 7 6 5 4 3 2 1

Manufactured in Guangdong, China CC062025